NASCAR RACERS

OFFICIAL
OWNER'S MANUAL

Written by Mel Gilden

HarperEntertainment
An Imprint of HarperCollins*Publishers*

HarperEntertainment
An Imprint of HarperCollins*Publishers*
10 East 53rd Street, New York, NY 10022-5299

First printing: May 2000
Cover illustration by Mel Grant
Designed by Susan Sanguily

Printed in the United States of America
ISBN 0-06-107181-1
HarperCollins®, ®, and HarperEntertainment™ are trademarks of HarperCollins Publishers Inc.
Visit HarperEntertainment on the World Wide Web at www.harpercollins.com
10 9 8 7 6 5 4 3 2 1

■ The Sponsor: **JACK FASSLER**

Foreword: Welcome to all drivers of the new NASCAR Unlimited Division Racing Cars. By Jack Fassler, Owner and Operator of Team Fastex.

NASCAR racing has always been an exciting sport. But with the new millennium come new technologies, new possibilities, and new challenges. The Unlimited Division of NASCAR embodies all that—and more.

The new cars—with their electronic enhancements, computer assistance, deployable lifting surfaces, and jet power—will require brave, intelligent, and talented men and women such as you to drive them. This Owner's Manual is designed to introduce you to the world of Unlimited racing. We want you to understand the facts you'll need to know and the skills you'll need to learn before you can join Team Fastex.

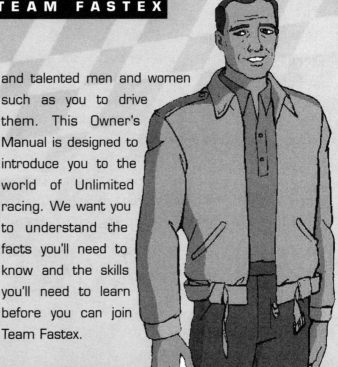

One way we'll do this is by taking a close look at Mark "Charger" McCutchen and his Team Fastex car. Charger is one of the finest drivers in the Unlimited Division, and his car is one of the most incredible speed machines ever seen in the NASCAR circuit. He comes from a long line of racing professionals, but it takes more than good genes to be a good Unlimited driver. Tomorrow's winning drivers could come from anywhere. The young man or woman I am looking for could be you!

While you study this Owner's Manual, keep in mind one thing—that no matter how impressive the cars are, they are only as good as their drivers.

Jack Fassler

What to expect when you drive for Jack Fassler:

Jack Fassler is the founder, owner, and main force behind Team Fastex and Unlimited Division racing. He started out in business as Garner Rexton's partner, but Rexton became increasingly shady in his business practices. Eventually he forced Fassler out of the business they had built together.

Fassler knows his business backward and forward, inside and out, and he prides himself on the fact that he can do any job on the Fastex Team. He could be his own crew chief if necessary, and has enough knowledge of computers to debug the training simulator. After his daughter, Megan, Team Fastex is the most important thing in Jack Fassler's life. He will do almost anything to protect it.

The conception and creation of New Motor City and the Motorsphere:

Conceived by Jack Fassler and built under his direction, New Motor City is on the banks of a great river somewhere in the American Midwest and is a paradise for anyone interested in auto racing—from the most casual fan to the most experienced driver.

Fassler's concerns with maintaining and improving the environment are apparent in all of his designs. His cars and garages generate the least possible amount of air, water, and ground pollution, and New Motor City recycles whatever it can. Work areas are designed for ease of use. When designing seating areas, refreshment stands, the entrances and exits, and even the restrooms, Fassler was determined to incorporate the most modern theories of people management into New Motor City.

New Motor City is something of an experiment in the world of racing, and many big corporations that might have been helpful to Fassler hesitated to get involved. For this reason, the stakes are even higher than they might be otherwise. Without the backing of other corporations, Fassler was forced to borrow money. Unfortunately, the bank that issued Jack Fassler a loan—Enormabanc—was bought by Jack's enemy, Garner Rexton. If Unlimited Division racing is not the success Fassler hopes it will be, he will lose everything to Rexton. Fassler will be broke and the city will be an empty monument to his aspirations.

Big River Raceway is the centerpiece of New Motor City, and the site of the first and last races of the Unlimited Division season.

Garner Rexton

5

MEET YOUR TEAMMATES

JACK FASSLER has put together one of the finest racing teams in the world. Now that you are a member of Team Fastex, it would be a good idea to get to know the other drivers.

■ Mark McCutchen, known as CHARGER

Charger was born in Mobile, Alabama. He has a short brush of blond hair and slate-gray eyes. Racing is in Charger's blood; his family has been in NASCAR for three generations. Charger's grandfather, Mack, had more than thirty wins in his NASCAR career. Junior McCutcheon, Charger's father, drove modifieds and sprint cars for years, and had just begun racing for NASCAR when his life was taken by a plane crash in the wilds of Alaska, ten years before Charger began his career. Charger has one brother, Miles. Charger's mother encourages her sons to do well, and takes pride in their accomplishments.

Charger has been racing all his life, starting with go-carts at the age of six. Like his father, Charger drives car number 204.

Though he is fair and sportsmanlike during a race, occasionally during a virtual training session Charger will imitate a Rexcor stunt, such as The Collector's attempt to push his opponents off the road.

Charger is likely to act before he thinks. He drives intuitively, by the seat of his pants. The ultimate competitor, Charger will accept any dare or challenge. In fact, Charger's nickname stems from the fact that he is the kind of person who is likely to charge into a situation rather than thinking through his actions first. Charger has a sense of humor about this personality trait. Whenever he is about to make his move during a race or take part in some other important or dangerous action, he will say, "Let's get charged!"

■ Megan Fassler, known as **SPITFIRE**

As the daughter of Jack Fassler, the founder and president of Fastex, she may someday be the company's head. As an automotive engineer, Megan designed the Team Fastex cars, but she longed to be a driver, a fact she kept from her father as long as she could. Her father, knowing the dangers involved in racing, tried to convince Megan that races are won in the garage, but "Spitfire" wanted to be in the middle of the racing action.

Spitfire is as hard on herself as she can be on others, and sometimes her biting wit is misunderstood by those around her. Because she has an intimate understanding of the car she drives, she can push it to its theoretical limit and beyond.

■ Steve Sharp, known as **FLYER**

Before becoming a driver for Team Fastex, Sharp was an Air Force captain flying fighter jets in combat. He is also trained in hand-to-hand combat.

Following a raid on a bio-chemical weapons factory, "Flyer" became prone to panic attacks, which caused him to suddenly quit the military.

Flyer eventually learned that his fear was not psychological, but chemically induced. Flyer is determined to overcome his fear, and refuses to allow his attacks to keep him from racing.

Flyer approaches racing as a second chance to test himself against other drivers, and other powerful machines. But he's hedging his bet. He knows that if necessary, he can drop out of a race, but he couldn't have dropped out of a battle. Flyer's approach to racing is cool and disciplined, just as his approach to flying in combat was.

■ Carlos Rey, known as **STUNTS**.

Stunts sees racing as a crowd-pleasing entertainment event, with drivers, owners, sponsors, and fans all contributing to create the sport.

When he was a kid, his parents started their own small business. But despite their hard work, it failed. This experience made Stunts impatient. He is unwilling to put off having fun or success. He is determined to find big financial success as early in his life as possible, and he sees NASCAR driving as his method of achieving that success.

But Stunts doesn't want money just for money's sake. Should he become the tycoon he wants to be, Stunts will be pleased to share his wealth with friends, family, and good causes.

Stunts is popular with his friends, fans, and family, not only because he is generous, but also because he is fun to be around and very loyal. He is slow to anger and has a wonderful sense of humor, which can lighten any situation.

Stunts is a natural driver as well as a natural showman, driving almost as though a race is a game. Following a crash, he's willing to reassure the crowd, especially its female members, that he is all right. He sometimes miffs other drivers when he shows off, because even when playing to the crowd he often wins his race. He enjoys racing motorcycles "for some real excitement."

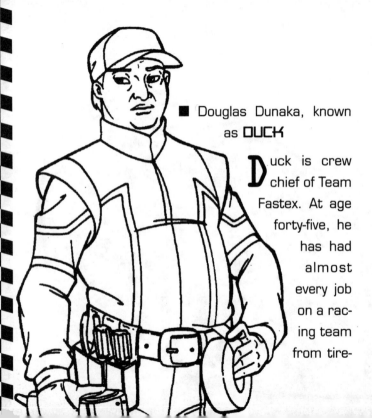

■ Douglas Dunaka, known as **DUCK**

Duck is crew chief of Team Fastex. At age forty-five, he has had almost every job on a racing team from tire-changer to driver, and he knows everything about cars and racing history. His crew includes mechanics, spotters, tire-changers, and fuelers.

One of Duck's many jobs is to double-check the circuits of the onboard computers before each race. Neither Fassler nor Dunaka are willing to trust anyone else with this task, because the computer system of each car is responsible not only for the smooth running of the car, but for the safety of the driver. Computers are responsible for monitoring everything from the correct air/fuel mixture in the engine to the deployment of the impact foam during a collision.

Duck frequently has a pessimistic outlook on events and he sometimes shows a prickly personality. He has an almost supernatural belief in the usefulness of duct tape, which he calls "duck tape." (This is the source of

Duck's nickname.) Sometimes, when working on a difficult job, he will tape the tools he is using against a convenient wall with duct tape, just to have them handy.

Like any professional mechanic, Duck owns his own tools. His toolbox is really more of a tool *cabinet*, as it is the size of a small upright piano. It is motorized and controlled by a small box about the size of a transistor radio. Control of the tool cabinet can be tricky, and occasionally when self-propelled it may run into objects.

His twelve-year-old daughter Shelby is interested in racing only as art and spectacle. Duck is tolerant of her attitude, though he is disappointed that she is not interested in cars as mechanical wonders.

THREE

CHARGER'S CAR

■ Mark "**CHARGER**" McCutchen is one of the finest drivers in racing, and has an equally fine automobile at his service. You will be driving his Unlimited Division car, so you'd better get to know everything you can about it. In some ways his car is very much like all the others in the Unlimited Division. But it also has some surprising differences.

General features of all Unlimited Division cars:

L ong before each season begins, every team is told what courses will be run, and what challenges the drivers will face. Each car is designed and built to have the same range of capabilities, but engineers work on details to suit the needs and talents of the individual drivers.

For example, Stunts can be a show-off, so Megan and Duck have given his car jets that allow it to ride on two wheels when necessary. This is useful when Stunts wants to get by two cars that are driving too closely together for him to pass under ordinary circumstances. He pulls the signature move handle and he speeds by on two wheels!

Unlimited Division cars are constructed of strong but lightweight materials. Special metals, plastics, rubbers, and ceramics all do their jobs.

Small but sturdy onboard computers help control

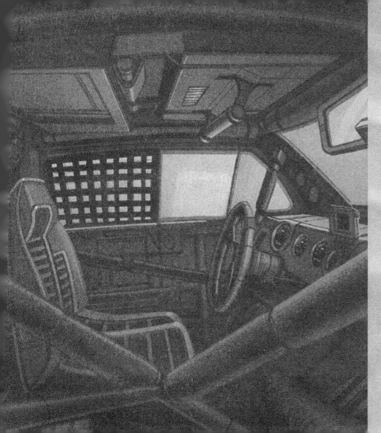

fuel mixtures and make minor adjustments in the engine as demands change. When a car is racing to pass another car, it needs a richer fuel mixture—higher-octane gasoline—than it would if it was moving at a steady clip or idling. If the engine is getting hot, the car's computer increases the activity of the cooling system.

Despite the lightweight materials used, all the additional accessories Unlimited Division cars are equipped with cause them to weigh a lot more than ordinary cars. (Each is heavy enough to bend the barrel of a tank gun!) But they also have improved handling and safety features as well as engines with bigger displacements and higher compression. This means that Unlimited Division cars can reach speeds of up to 400 miles per hour on a super-speedway.

Team Fastex crew chief, Duck Dunaka, sometimes worries that the Unlimited Division's new forced combustion carburetors will overheat. Forced combustion is one of several methods of adding performance to an engine by forcing air into the carburetor. It is an updated method of turbocharging or supercharging.

In high heat conditions, heat sensors should shut down the engine before the situation becomes explosive. In addition, Megan's design has adjusted the carburetor in such a way that it should no longer overheat.

However, if Megan's modifications are tampered with, the carburetor is still susceptible to overheating. It can be heartbreaking if the car shuts down during a race. This once happened to Charger, but he kept his head and won the race by pushing his car across the finish line. Lucky for Charger, all the other cars on the track were in worse shape than his was!

But remember, despite all these fancy modifications, the single most important part of an Unlimited Division racer is still the driver.

MEET YOUR CAR

You'll be driving Charger's Unlimited Division racer. What follows are all the facts you'll need to know so you can handle this incredible machine like a pro!

■ The Cab

The window on the driver's side is a flap that can be opened and closed manually. This is the driver's normal place of entry and exit.

Car cabs are reinforced to help the driver withstand the normal knocks, shocks, and vibrations that he or she will suffer under racing conditions—so you shouldn't get too knocked around!

Pedals, Levers, and Instruments

The arrangement of foot pedals: gas, brake, and clutch are right to left, as in conventional street vehicles. In Team Fastex cars, the starter is a button on the dashboard to the left of the steering wheel. No key is necessary to start the car.

The *gearshift lever*, for changing gears, is floor-mounted. Generally, instruments are circular. One of the gauges nearest the driver, just to the right of the steering wheel, displays the engine temperature. Under extreme conditions a color bar at the top of the instrument will flash red. If nothing is done to decrease the engine's temperature, the glass over the instrument will crack. Another instrument is the *tachometer*, which displays how fast the engine is turning over in revolutions per minute.

A *jump lever*, located on the floor on the right side of the seat, activates rockets for short jumps over opponents, crashes, obstacles, and holes in the road.

Air Temperature Regulation and Life Support

Under racing conditions, air temperature regulation is not a luxury—it's a necessity. The driving suits are insulated, and air is forced onto the driver from all sides—cold air in hot climates and warm air in cold climates.

Through gear in their helmets, drivers are in constant communication with other members of their team—the pit crew, fellow drivers, and observers in the communications room of the hauler.

On the center console is a button that can shut down the engine in case of emergency. But if the

heat sensors are disabled or tampered with, the forced combustion carburetors may overheat, causing the throttle to stick in an open position. When the engine is in this extreme condition it *cannot be shut down*. Worse yet, the heat will become critical long before the car runs out of fuel. As it reaches a critical condition, flames begin to shoot out of the glowing red carburetor. All you can do at this point is downshift, head for daylight, and deploy the Rescue Racer. Remember: *At this point your vehicle is about to explode!* You must launch your *Rescue Racer* (explained later in the book) at top speed in order to outrace the fireball caused by the explosion.

Other systems such as the *impact foam delivery system* also help save the life of the driver in emergencies.

■ Monitors

Because the cars go so fast in quickly changing situations and road conditions, it is very important that you are constantly aware of your surroundings while you are driving. Therefore, instead of a rearview mirror, your Unlimited Division racer is equipped with a *TV monitor*. Using this feature you may see what is behind, what is on either side, or even above your vehicle.

Every car is also equipped with a camera inside the cab that records the actions of the driver. These records are a handy training material. They can be viewed later by the driver and other team members to observe what the driver does under certain circumstances.

■ Signature Move Handle

As a Team Fastex driver, you will have your own "signature move"—a characteristic maneuver that only your car can do, activated by a *signature move handle*. Signature moves generally involve an unusual use of rockets and wings, either deployed alone or in combination.

A "signature move handle" which is parallel to the windshield and hangs from the ceiling of the cab, where it can be easily reached by the driver's right hand, deploys each signature move. To activate it, the driver pulls it down. To deactivate, the driver pushes it back toward the ceiling of the cab.

It is a good idea to know the signature moves used by your teammates as well as your own. This will give you a better chance of working together in tense racing situations.

a. Charger's "signature move," the special ability built into the car you will be driving, is to fire booster jets which slide out from each side of his car and also blast from the undercarriage of the front of his car. The jets will allow you to maneuver quickly.

b. Flyer's "signature move" is to make delta wings pop out from the undercarriage sides of the car, and booster jets fire from the rear of his car. This allows Flyer to sail over cars ahead of him.

c. Stunts's "signature move" is the ability to use jets in the undercarriage to tilt the car up on two wheels on the same side, allowing it to pass another car or obstacle in a narrow space.

d. Spitfire's "signature move" is to deploy rockets, which expand from the sides of her car, increasing her speed considerably.

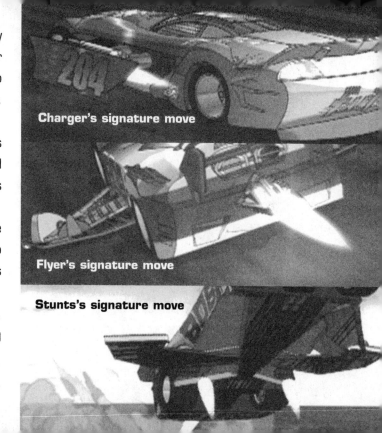

Charger's signature move

Flyer's signature move

Stunts's signature move

Impact Foam

Deployment of impact foam is automatic, activated by sensors throughout the car. Like an airbag, impact foam fills the driver's compartment if the car crashes. It enters the cab through the hub of the steering wheel, through vents in the door, and behind the driver's head. The foam becomes rigid instantly upon contact with the air, encasing the driver in a protective shell. Seconds later it disintegrates, allowing the driver to exit the car or operate the Rescue Racer.

■ Color Scheme

The interior surfaces of the Team Fastex cabs are mostly black. However, each driver has a distinctive color scheme. You will be driving Charger's car, which has a red scheme. Flyer's car has a blue scheme, Stunts's car has a green scheme, and Spitfire's car has a purple scheme.

■ Lights

All cars have both headlights and taillights for safety in tunnels and on night runs. There's no need to turn on the lights. Sensors in the roof of your car will activate head- and taillights when the environment turns dark, as in a tunnel or at night.

■ Wings and Spoilers

Aerodynamic panels are sophisticated *spoilers* that can be used as wings in emergencies or to gain a racing advantage. They can be deployed either automatically or by the driver. Automatic deployment occurs when sensors feel the car is not steady on the road and it requires a stabilizing influence. Spoilers can also be used as rudders to help steer the car, as braking mechanisms, or as wings that allow the car to fly for a few hundred feet.

■ Jets and Rockets

All boosters and jets must be used sparingly because they take a lot of fuel to run. If you use them too often, you will find yourself hitting the pits to refuel and will lose any advantage gained. Also, there is always a chance that, as it lands, a flying car will accidentally bump a car on the road. In this case, the car may spin or bounce out of control, possibly causing the spoilers or the impact foam to deploy.

Turbojet boosters are small jet engines built into the car to give it greater speed when not touching the ground—as when the aerodynamic panels are engaged—or when running on a slick surface such as ice. Front boosters can aid in braking.

Rocket boosters are similar to turbojet boosters but are technically somewhat different. They may be used when the car is still rolling on the ground. These can also be useful getting out of sandpits and other similar traps.

Control jets are smaller boosters located on the corners of each car. These can be used to enhance control or regain control.

When you are driving Charger's car, you can move the side rockets back into the body of the car by pushing a switch above the signature handle and then pushing the jump lever forward. Immediately, rockets will fire from a triangular-shaped vent on each side of the car. This *vent rocket* will allow you to move the racer strongly sideways, perhaps to prevent another car from passing.

SPECIAL FEATURES

■ Signature Move

Use Charger's signature move handle to fire booster jets, which slide out from each side of the car and also blast from the undercarriage of the front of the car. The jets can greatly increase the speed of Charger's car, but you must not forget that the side jets are comparatively fragile, and can be sheared off if they hit the sidewall of the track.

■ Structural Integrity

The structure of the car and its suspension systems can withstand hard knocks, such as being bumped from the side by another car or

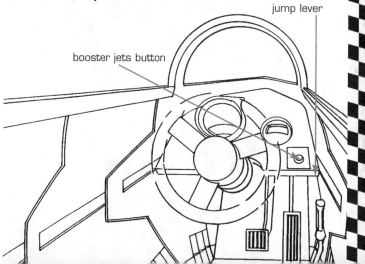

jump lever

booster jets button

being caught between two cars. However, if one car lands on the roof of another too hard, the bottom car may suffer a cracked windshield.

■ Special Equipment

Special equipment can be added for off-road races— sharp blades in jungles, or baffles to keep out sand on desert courses. Megan and Duck usually install these accessories.

A switch above the windshield, behind the signature move handle, opens a small door in the hood and fires a grappling hook. With the help of studs on the morphing tires which give the car extra traction, the hook is strong enough to pull a helicopter out of the sky.

For off-road races, each car carries a *Global Positioning System* which receives satellite signals that give the car's exact location. An onboard computer map shows each driver where he or she is. It also shows team members aboard the hauler the locations of the other cars on their team. For the Tundra 2000, both Team Fastex and Team Rexcor cars were equipped with snowplows that could be deployed with the flick of a switch. Also for the Tundra 2000, Flyer's car was equipped with a double buzz saw—twin rotating circular blades which were used to cut down trees, thus clearing a path through a forest. The blades were at the ends of arms that came out from under the front of the car. The switch to deploy this was located on the left above the windshield.

■ Rescue Racer

The *Rescue Racer* is another safety feature unique to Unlimited Division cars. It is a very compact, self-contained vehicle built into the main car with its own wheels and a smaller engine. In emergency

Flyer's double buzz saw

situations you will be glad it's available to you. You have the option of arming explosive bolts and releasing couplings, allowing the Rescue Racer to be ejected from your damaged full-size car. If a driver uses a Rescue Racer during the last lap of a race, he or she may cross the finish line in it.

On Team Fastex Unlimited Division cars, the handle deploying the rescue racer is a bar on the dashboard similar to the one above the windshield which controls the signature move. *Remembering where it is could save your life!*

Pulling the bar down instantly pops the car's canopy, allowing the rescue racer to be ejected, leaving the main car to its fiery fate. After the rescue racer is in the air, the driver pulls back a lever in the center console, deploying the wings.

Take care, because deploying the rescue racer wings may sometimes flip the rescue racer over, so that it is flying upside-down. If that happens, you may push a button on your main dashboard to fire booster jets—one firing from above the wing, the other from below—which will flip the rescue racer over so that it is right side up.

The rescue racer is also equipped with impact foam, which will deploy automatically under sufficiently critical conditions.

The structure of the rescue racer is sturdy enough to protect the driver in whatever attitude it hits the ground, right side up or upside down. If struck hard enough, the canopy will shatter. Please note: Rescue racers were not originally designed to float. However, they have recently been modified so they can float, but are not very maneuverable in fast-moving water.

Charger's rescue racer has a rectangular air intake at the front. It has two small wheels in the front at the ends of outriggers, and one wheel in the back. Four exhaust pipes erupt from either side of the structure behind the head area. It is equipped with brake lights.

■ Drogue Chute

A *drogue chute* is a parachute that can be deployed from the rear of the car to help with braking. After use, it can be released from the car. However, releasing a chute can be dangerous to a following car because the chute can cover that car's windshield. The drogue chute can be used only once in a race.

■ Morphing Tires

Morphing tires can grow special tread configurations, bumps, and patterns on the driver's demand to match specific road conditions. For instance, you may deploy studs in dusty or sandy conditions. These can also be useful in getting out of sandpits and other similar traps.

To make spikes protrude from your tires, push the switch behind the signature move handle over the windshield. A similar switch will cause the tires to corrugate (wrinkle), allowing your car to get better traction on icy surfaces. Morphing tires are well tested before they are used in a race. (In early tests, the spikes dug up the track too much. On retraction, the test car flipped over. However, this problem has been

corrected, and morphing tires may now be used safely in an off-road race.)

The tires normally used on the cars smoke against the track on jackrabbit starts and with sudden braking. They are made out of material very much like the high-grade rubber out of which today's NASCAR tires are made. Note: *Sharp objects can puncture the tires.*

Driving suits are designed both to protect the driver and to easily identify him or her. Your driving suit will have all the safety features of other Team Fastex driving suits, and icons and colors that will be yours alone.

COLORS AND ICONS

Each driver on Team Fastex has his or her own colors and icons. The driving suits are individually designed to match the driver's style, and you will soon be getting one of your own.

Charger's driving suit is red with yellow accents. On his chest is emblazoned a stylized drawing of a knight charging into battle.

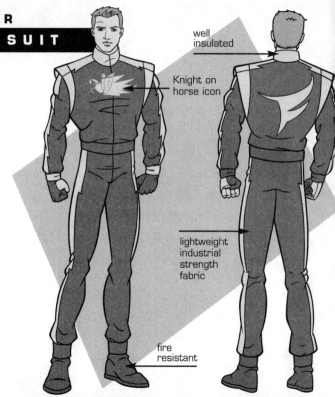

well insulated

Knight on horse icon

lightweight industrial strength fabric

fire resistant

CAPABILITIES

All driving suits are fire-resistant. Helmets are air-cooled and contain communications gear. Using this gear, drivers may speak with each other as well as with members of their pit crew. When not inside a car, a driver may speak to base using a small handheld auxiliary radio.

A strong swimmer may swim in his or her suit. After climbing from freezing water and walking around in deep snow, a Team Fastex driver will show no evidence of freezing, or of even being cold. Tests show that the suits are even better insulated than Jack Fassler expected.

Though talent is an important part of what makes an Unlimited Division driver successful, you must have other attributes as well—tenacity and technique. Tenacity is important because even a talented driver cannot succeed unless he or she is willing to spend time at the track practicing driving skills and preparing for emergencies. Good driving must become second nature. Perfection of technique comes with practice. Team Fastex uses two main types of race training: live and virtual.

LIVE

Built shortly after the turn of the millennium, Big River Raceway—a complex of drag strips, speedways, parking areas, viewing stands, and garages—is the final word in car racing architecture.

The most fantastic feature of Big River Raceway is the Motorsphere. Inside, a number of track and weather conditions may be artificially created.

Access roads allow drivers, crews, and raceway maintenance people to drive quickly and easily from one location inside it to another. One can also turn off the main track onto the main access road. The infield track is skirted by a jogging track. In the center of the infield is an ornamental lake with a roadway over it. On race days the infield is crowded with recreational vehicles.

Fastex Headquarters Tunnel Entrance

Spotted around the tracks are computer-controlled cameras that record everything a Team Fastex car and driver do. These records are viewed later to help you and your team members to train, plan strategy, and avoid making the same errors again.

VIRTUAL

Megan "Spitfire" Fassler invented the training simulator, a sophisticated motion simulator—the next generation following the simulators seen in late twentieth century. If a simulation is stopped while a driver hangs upside down in his rescue racer, the driver will find himself upside down in the motion simulator after the simulation stops.

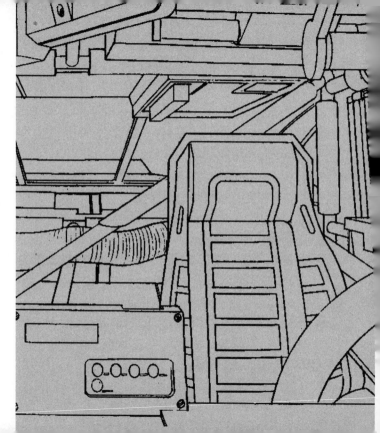

Simulator Interior

Megan occasionally must remind drivers, who are naturally competitive, that, "The virtual reality simulator isn't a computer game. It's a training tool for a completely new form of NASCAR racing."

Four trainers are kept in the simulation room of the training building, Building T67. It is an enormous hut-shaped building with buttresses that start about two-thirds of the way up the wall and support a ring which runs around the entire top of the building. Each simulator sits on the floor of the simulator room, and is connected to a master computer by heavy cables, which hang from the ceiling. A giant number (1 through 4) is printed on the outside of each simulator. Simulator #4 is closest to the command center.

Using a combination of computer-generated images timed perfectly with computer controlled motion, a

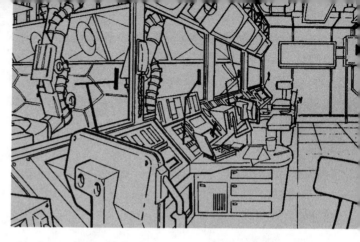

simulator realistically reproduces the NASCAR driving experience—the heart-stopping speed, the feel of the car and the track, the noise and heat in the vehicle, and the effects of draft on speed and handling. The simulated view of the world outside is projected directly onto the training car's windows.

A driver may ask the simulator to deliver any sort of driving situation, from the most basic to the most complex and difficult. As the simulator accepts the commands, the dashboard instruments light up. Simulated vehicles sometimes seem to be racing without a driver at the wheel. In addition, the virtual projection is not limited to the inside of the car. The simulations are so complete that the driver may exit his or her car in the virtual world and still remain in the simulation.

The simulator is not programmed with the signature moves of Team Fastex. However, the simulator can reproduce emergency situations such as those requiring usage of a rescue racer.

The simulator command room has the look of the control center of a space launch. In it, one can look down upon the simulators through large windows.

On screens in the simulator command room, observers can see what the drivers see. The screens can also replay simulations, and access complete dossiers on drivers or other personnel.

The simulator computer accepts verbal commands in the command center or in any of the simulators. Diagnostic functions can also be initiated verbally, and the computer will answer the same way.

When a simulation has been stopped or is concluded, the driver touches a control which motivates the hydraulics that lift the transparent canopy. The driver releases his safety harness, climbs out of the cab, and steps onto the floor of the simulation room.

Dirty Drivers and Their Dirty Tricks

As an Unlimited Division driver, you'll be racing against the best of the best—and the worst of the worst! Here are some low-down moves to look out for—and how to handle them.

■ Garner Rexton: **THE BOSS**

Rexton is a genius who is determined to get his revenge against Jack Fassler. Though they were once partners who built a business together, Rexton soon took the business away from Fassler by underhanded means. Now he and Jack Fassler are fiercely competitive.

Rexton wants to destroy Team Fastex, and he feels the best way to do that is to ensure that Fassler loses the first season of Unlimited Division racing. He'll stop at nothing to get his revenge, even going as far as allowing his drivers to injure Fassler's daughter Megan during a race.

Rexton has assembled a skilled racing team whose members are as mean and liable to cheat as he is, but he looks forward to the day when he won't need drivers at all.

The Team Rexcor drivers know a library of dirty tricks that they will commit when they have the opportunity. Noted below are just a few of the worst. *Studying the methods of the Team Rexcor drivers, knowing what they might do, can save your life and the lives of your teammates.*

■ Lyle Owens, known as **THE COLLECTOR**

Owens got his nickname because he is known to cause accidents and then collect souvenirs from them.

"The Collector" feels that he is unlucky, and blames his failures on others. He pretends to be a good teammate and can be genuinely charming. He befriends young drivers and then betrays them, telling lies and spreading rumors. He has a wide jealous streak and dislikes seeing men, particularly Charger, talking to Megan Fassler.

In the early stages of the Unlimited Division, he got a ride with Team Fastex, but was fired for dirty driving. At the time, no one at Team Fastex realized that Owens was a spy for Team Rexcor.

One of The Collector's favorite dirty tricks is to

rise into the air using his jump lever or signature move handle, and then come down hard on an opposing vehicle. However, it is possible for him to come down *too* hard. In that case, his jet engines may suddenly close up into his car, causing it to spin out of control.

Using a button on an array above the windshield, he can open a small pair of sliding doors in the front of his car and release an arrowlike grappling hook, which when fired at another car can cause an instant blowout in one of its tires. The best defense against this dirty trick is to stay out of The Collector's way. Failing that, your options are limited. You may drive to the nearest pit or IMP, or you may be forced to eject in your rescue racer.

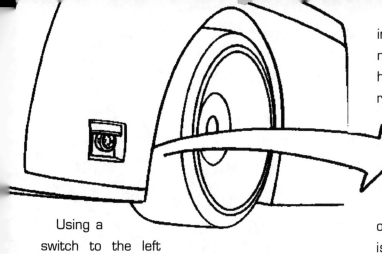

incorrect reading of the racecourse. A driver will not necessarily immediately realize that the scrambler has affected his computer. However, the scrambled racecourse computer image may be so wrong that the driver can't help but notice. For instance, it might cause the computer to display a grid of San Diego when one is in Alaska.

The dashboard of The Collector's car is also equipped with a video screen used to communicate with Garner Rexton. The other Team Rexcor racers are similarly equipped.

Using a switch to the left above the windshield, The Collector may launch a small object like a Japanese throwing star from his front fender. This object is a scrambler. It is designed to fly across the open space between cars, attach itself to the target car, and at the flick of a switch, cause the target car's computer to give an

45

■ Hondo Hines, known as **SPECTER**

Specter is a skillful driver who has an eerie threatening calm. He makes his move when least expected, appearing suddenly, like a ghost or specter, and striking swiftly, wrecking the competition. Though he claims to have smiled in his life, no one has ever actually seen him do it. He sees himself as cool, and often wears sunglasses, even when the sun isn't shining.

A compulsive gambler, Specter will bet on anything, and sometimes pays off debts by doing a "little job" for people he owes money to. These "jobs" are usually illegal.

Specter and his Team Rexcor teammate Junker sometimes work together against a driver from an opposing team. They will drive far enough apart to allow the opposing driver between them and then suddenly swerve together, slamming the opposing car. A good defense for this move is a technique invented by Charger: a sudden slowdown, so that the two Rexcor vehicles speed ahead and slam into each other.

■ ZORINA

Vain, intelligent, and beautiful, Zorina is a former model with alternative rock music tastes. Into bodybuilding, Zorina likes to show off her muscles. "Been there, done that" personified, she is in racing for the kicks and the attention of the crowd.

One of her favorite dirty tricks is to *ram* an opposing car from the side, often using a switch on her center console to activate jets that push her to the side with even greater force. She does this maneuver in an attempt to bump competing cars off the track, but it often causes her car to spin out, requiring her to deploy her rescue racer.

■ Diesel Spitz, known as JUNKER

He has a bad reputation and is rumored to have a criminal record in Europe. He enjoys wrecking his car and the cars of others. In fact, he was the top-rated driver in Europe until he started wrecking every car he drove. The bigger the crash, the more he enjoyed it. If he's not in a crash he may take a sledgehammer to his car and smash it just for fun.

One of Junker's favorite tricks is to drop parts of his car—fenders, quarter panels, tailpipes, or other pieces of expendable metal—turning the track into an obstacle course. The best defense against this trick is to stay alert, always ready to avoid or jump over the stray dangerous road trash he creates.

To gain an advantage, Junker will leave the track, even cutting across country through stands of trees, rocks, and gullies.

By flipping a switch just to the right of the shift lever, he can open a hatch on the hood of his car and fire a pair of grappling hooks. The cable attached to the grappling hooks is strong enough to briefly support the weight of his race car.

A lever similar to a hood release is under his dashboard, reachable by his right hand. Pulling it causes one of his own rear tires to blow, making his car swerve across the track, becoming an obstacle to the other cars in the race. One way to avoid crashing into Junker's car is to use the jump lever and fly over the whole mess.

■ SPEX

This part human, part cybernetic construct is Team Rexcor's Chief Engineer. Nobody knows his real name or who he was before. He is very strong, has unnaturally sharp hearing, and speaks in a frightening electronic voice. When looking for something, he sees by means of a Terminator-style targeting device.

His bionic parts contain hidden equipment. For example, his left arm contains a small blowtorch and an electronic probe on a cable which can be extended from his body. The wrist of his left hand hides a pneumatic wrench which uses high-pressure blasts of air.

Spex is not without his weaknesses. If one is trapped in the grasp of Spex's arms, the victim may use a socket wrench to ratchet a gear on Spex's back. This will cause Spex's bionic arms to involuntarily rise into the air. Using the same technique, the arms can be lowered into their normal position.

It is said that Garner Rexton can see and hear everything Spex sees and hears, and Rexton frequently speaks to his team or visitors over the video hook-up on Spex's chest. By unfolding a keyboard from an area just below the screen, Spex can activate and control Rexton's secret weapons.

SEVEN

A race is the car's ultimate test. Or as Duck might say, "The proof of the car is in the racing." Not only must you and your car be in top condition, but it is important that you be familiar with any track or course you race on.

NASCAR drivers compete for championship points. The winner of a race wins the most points, the runner-up wins a slightly lower number of points, and so on down to the fourth runner-up. Therefore, finishing in the top five is worth almost as much as winning, so while winning an individual race is important, your runner-up points accumulate as the season continues. Your overall season track record determines your standing in the division. It is far better to be a runner-up consistently than to win a few races and not place in the top five for the rest.

Before the start of a race, the cars drive slowly around the track behind a pace car, which keeps them in formation until the signal to start the race is given. At Big River Raceway, a video flag, a huge blank video screen mounted above the starting line, gives the signal. When a *green* flag appears on the screen, the race begins. A *yellow* flag appearing on the screen, along with flashing lights, indicates that drivers should exercise caution, for example, if debris is on the track. Cars may not pass each other during a yellow flag condition. A *red* flag on the electronic flag board is the signal to stop the race. This may happen if the track becomes blocked or a condition exists that makes the race impossible to continue.

A tall position tower shows the lap number to the crowd.

The winner of a race is immediately announced on an electronic screen at the finish line, where a sensor reads a coded transmitter signal in the nose of the car, determining the winner. The name of the winner appears on the screen with the traditional *checkered flag*. The winning car then drives onto the Victory Lane.

Races are either *speedway* or *off-road*. Off-road races take place at exotic venues all over the world. For example, the Desert 500 is driven in

the country Secado (which means "dry" in Spanish).

Team Fastex also competes in the Tundra 2000, a race through the Alaskan backcountry. Because of its cold, snow, and freezing road conditions, the Tundra 2000 is considered one of the most grueling races on the Unlimited Division calendar. On such cross-country races there are checkpoints at various locations along the route.

Unlimited Division racing is not just a competition but a sort of laboratory to test new automobile technology. The "exotic" piece of equipment an Unlimited Division car uses may become standard equipment on all cars in the future.

■ The Motorsphere

The Motorsphere is the ultimate training ground and is tremendously useful to Team Fastex. Challenging and exciting, drivers return to it again and again to test their skills. Inside, a variety of track and weather conditions can be artificially created.

Because the cars go so fast inside the Motorsphere, centrifugal force enables them to do one of the more astonishing maneuvers in racing, even in Unlimited Division racing. The cars can race up the sidewalls and across the top of the structure, racing upside down! "Centrifugal" literally means "fleeing the center." You can see this force in action by tying an eraser or other small object to the end of a string and then swinging the object in a circle.

The object pulls the string tight because it is "fleeing the center." The speed at which the Unlimited Division cars go up the side of the Motorsphere causes the same effect, and pushes the car against the track—even when the track is on the ceiling!

Entry into the Motorsphere is through a short tunnel.

Enormous screens on the inside surface can show track action.

■ Pit Area and Garages

The pit area has almost one hundred bays extending along one side of the track. It has its own loading zone, where a hauler can pick up and drop off cars, and anything from a spark plug to a new engine may be delivered. Large video screens over the pit area show what is happening on any part of the track.

The Team Fastex pit area is not to be confused with the Team Fastex garage, where even more complex operations may be done. The Team Fastex garage is clean and well stocked. Using its facilities, one can do anything from change a tire to rebuild an engine. At the rear of the big room are a number of computer terminals for use by the drivers and crew.

Over the stands across from the pit area is a line of luxury boxes, which provide a spectacular view of the racetracks.

■ Exotic Races

Examples of exotic speedway and off-road races include:

London to Paris, including a high-speed stretch through the Channel Tunnel. This is a lot more dan-

gerous than it sounds because the only track openings are at either end, so there is no pulling off into the pit or the infield during trouble. If a car in front of you has trouble, you must be able to speed past it. Trying to maneuver using a jump lever or signature move will be a problem because of the limited ceiling height.

A Death Valley race. This course has extreme heat conditions. Cars are in constant danger of overheating and of losing traction due to sand conditions.

A promotional race in which the drivers must finish the race in their rescue racers. If you encounter a situation where you would normally use the rescue racer to save your life, you have a choice to make—you can use the rescue racer at that time and know you've just lost the race, or you can come up with a more creative solution, risking death or serious injury, and save the rescue racer for the final lap of the race.

A night run on a street circuit through Manhattan. Even on a closed course, the city provides challenges that you would not meet on a racetrack built for that purpose. Pot holes, dips, and variable surfaces are just three of the problems you might meet.

A race on the deck of a scrapped aircraft carrier with spectators watching from cruise ships. Of course the danger here is that if you spin out, you might end up in the ocean.

An "auto steeplechase" on a special track equipped with loops, jumps, and pitfalls. This race is the ultimate test of your jumping and signature move abilities.

A race across the varied terrain of Peru, from the Amazon Jungle to the Andes Mountains. Contestants must constantly readjust their cars for altitude, temperature, and humidity.

A race on the Bonneville Salt Flats, with the longest

straightaway and highest speeds in NASCAR history. Higher speeds do not necessarily mean more danger, but the faster things happen, the more likely you are to find yourself in big trouble when there is any trouble at all. "Think fast" is more than just a slogan.

A midwinter race in St. Petersburg, Russia, across frozen Lake Ladoga. Cold and slick surfaces are obviously the problems here.

A race across the Sahara Desert, near the pyramids. Again, drivers will face heat conditions, plus the added challenge of racing on sand.

How well do you know your car and your new team? Find out by taking this quiz!

1. The Team Fastex Unlimited Simulator was invented by
   a. Jack Fassler
   b. "Duck" Dunaka
   c. Megan Fassler
   d. Miles McCutchen

2. Before he joined Team Fastex, Steve Sharp was employed as
   a. a professional boxer
   b. a military jet pilot
   c. a computer programmer
   d. a movie stuntman

3. The Signature Move handle is located
   a. on the floor to the right of the driver's seat
   b. on the ceiling where it can be easily reached by the driver's right hand.
   c. below the dashboard
   d. on the floor next to the brake pedal

4. Stunts's "signature move" is
   a. to go up on two wheels
   b. to move quickly sideways
   c. to fly for short distances
   d. to release a drogue chute

5. On Unlimited Division cars a small TV monitor replaces what is normally a
   a. front windshield
   b. rear window
   c. rearview mirror
   d. gas gauge

6. Under special circumstances a Team Fastex car might be equipped with which of these accessories?
   a. buzz saw blades
   b. a snowplow
   c. morphing tires
   d. all of the above

7. Onboard computers control
   a. air/fuel mixtures
   b. engine temperature
   c. deployment of impact foam
   d. all of the above

8. On a super-speedway Unlimited Division cars can reach
   a. 100 miles per hour
   b. 200 miles per hour
   c. 300 miles per hour
   d. 400 miles per hour

9. IMP means
   a. Independent Matrix Propulsion
   b. Integrated Micro Path
   c. Independently Mobile Pit
   d. Independent Mechanical Project

10. The tachometer measures
   a. engine temperature in degrees centigrade
   b. gas consumption in gallons per minute
   c. engine speed in revolutions per minute
   d. speed in miles per hour

HOW MANY DID YOU GET RIGHT?

8–10

LEVEL A: NASCAR UNLIMITED DIVISION SUPER-DRIVER. You're ready for the road! Level A means you're ready to take on even the most difficult off-road and superspeedway courses. So suit up and get behind the wheel of your supercar!

4–7

LEVEL B: NASCAR UNLIMITED DIVISION DRIVER. You've got the right stuff for standard speedway races, but you'll need another spin through this Owner's Manual before you're ready for the toughest courses. With a little more studying, you'll have your pedal to the metal in no time!

1–3

LEVEL C: NASCAR UNLIMITED DIVISION DRIVER-IN-TRAINING. You need a few hours in the simulator before you sit behind the wheel of Charger's speed machine. But don't give up! Remember that real drivers never quit, no matter how tough the course is!

NASCAR RACERS

Join the winner's circle! Enter to win this ultracool sweepstakes!

One lucky Grand Prize Winner, along with his or her parent or legal guardian,
will receive a FREE trip to the official NASCAR SpeedPark closest to his or her home!

TO ENTER: Send in a contest entry form located at the back of *NASCAR Racers #1: The Fast Lane*; *NASCAR Racers #2: Taking the Lead*; *NASCAR Racers: How They Work*; and *NASCAR Racers: Official Owner's Manual* OR send in a 3 X 5 card complete with your name, address, telephone number, and birthday to the address below.

Official Rules: No Purchase Necessary to enter or win a prize. This sweepstakes is open to U.S. residents 18 years and under as of September 1, 2000, except employees and their families of HarperCollins Publishers, NASCAR, Saban Entertainment, and their agencies, affiliates, and subsidiaries. This sweepstakes begins on April 1, 2000 and all entries must be received on or before September 1, 2000. HarperCollins Publishers is not responsible for late, lost, incomplete, or misdirected mail. Winners will be selected in a random drawing on or about September 1, 2000 and notified by mail shortly thereafter. Odds of winning depend on number of entries received. All entries become property of HarperCollins Publishers and will not be returned or acknowledged. Entry constitutes permission to use the winner's name, hometown, and likeness for promotional purposes on behalf of HarperCollins Publishers. To claim prize, winners must sign an Affidavit of Eligibility, Assignment and release within 10 days of notification, or another winner will be chosen. One Grand Prize of a free trip to the NASCAR SpeedPark closest to the winner's home will be awarded (approximate retail value, $2,000). HarperCollins Publishers will provide the sweepstakes winner and one parent or legal guardian with round-trip coach air transportation from major airport nearest winner to the NASCAR Speedpark closest to the winner's home, 2-day passes into the NASCAR SpeedPark and standard hotel accommodations for a two-night stay. Trip must be taken within one year from the date prize is awarded. Blackout dates and other restrictions may apply. All additional expenses are the responsibility of the prize winner. One entry per envelope. No facsimiles accepted.

Airline, hotel and all other travel arrangements will be made by HarperCollins Publishers in its discretion. HarperCollins Publishers reserves the right to substitute a cash payment of $2,000 for the Grand Prize. Travel and use of hotel and NASCAR SpeedPark are at risk of winner and neither HarperCollins Publishers nor NASCAR SpeedPark assumes any liability.

Sweepstakes void where prohibited. Applicable taxes are the sole responsibility of the winners. Prizes are not transferable and there will be no substitutions of the prizes except at the discretion of HarperCollins Publishers. For the name of the Grand Prize winner, send a self-addressed stamped envelope by October 1, 2000 to HarperCollins Publishers at the address listed to the left. VT and WA residents may omit return postage.

ENTER THE NASCAR SWEEPSTAKES:
Mail this entry form along with the following information to: **HarperCollins Publishers**
10 East 53rd Street
New York, NY 10022
Attn: Department LP

Name: _____

Address: _____

City: _____

State: _____ Zip: _____

Phone #:_____

Birthday: _____